THE GREEN TEAM

by Jon Mikkelsen
illustrated by Nathan Lueth

Librarian Reviewer
Marci Peschke
Librarian, Dallas Independent School District
MA Education Reading Specialist, Stephen F. Austin State University
Learning Resources Endorsement, Texas Women's University

Reading Consultant
Elizabeth Stedem
Educator/Consultant, Colorado Springs, CO
MA in Elementary Education, University of Denver, CO

STONE ARCH BOOKS
www.stonearchbooks.com

Keystone Books are published by Stone Arch Books
151 Good Counsel Drive, P.O. Box 669
Mankato, Minnesota 56002
www.stonearchbooks.com

Library of Congress Cataloging-in-Publication Data
Mikkelsen, Jon.
 The Green Team / by Jon Mikkelsen; illustrated by Nathan Lueth.
 p. cm. — (Keystone Books. We Are Heroes)
 ISBN 978-1-4342-0789-0 (library binding)
 ISBN 978-1-4342-0885-9 (pbk.)
 [1. Green movement—Fiction. 2. Self-actualization (Psychology)—
Fiction.] I. Lueth, Nathan, ill. II. Title.
PZ7.M59268Gr 2009
[Fic]—dc22   2008008118

Summary: Noah Green wants to plant trees at school, but will anyone
help him?

Art Directior Heather Kindseth
Graphic Designer: Brann Garvey

1 2 3 4 5 6 13 12 11 10 09 08

TABLE OF CONTENTS

Chapter 1
INVISIBLE...5

Chapter 2
IN THE SHADE 7

Chapter 3
A GREAT TEAM.................................. 14

Chapter 4
THE GREEN TEAM 18

Chapter 5
HELP FROM DAD................................. 24

Chapter 6
A TRUCKLOAD OF TREES 26

Chapter 1

Noah Green was sick and tired of being invisible.

He wasn't really invisible, but he felt like it sometimes when he was at school. Everyone seemed to ignore him.

Noah wasn't good at sports. He didn't get the best grades. He wasn't very popular. When other kids weren't ignoring him, they were picking on him and calling him names.

Noah was good at one thing. His dad owned a landscaping company, "Green Thumb Landscaping." Every summer, Noah helped his dad. He started helping his dad pick weeds when he was five.

Now, at age fourteen, he could do almost anything at his dad's company. He mowed lawns. He planted flowers and trees. He installed water fountains. He helped dig gardens.

The other people who worked at Green Thumb respected Noah. He felt proud of his work. He loved working outside in the sun with his dad. He loved being part of the Green Thumb team.

He just hated being at school.

Chapter 2

On Monday morning, Noah walked into his Social Studies class just as the bell rang. "Barely on time," Mr. Young said. "One second later and you'd have detention."

"Sorry," Noah said. He quickly sat down.

Mr. Young said, "Okay, class. I told you last week that today we'd talk about your semester project."

"What is it?" a girl asked. "Is it a research paper?"

"No," Mr. Young said. "It's a project. It will count for half of your grade. For this project, you will need to do one thing to help the community."

"I want to help the community by adding more vending machines in the cafeteria!" said Ethan.

Ethan was on the football team. All the girls liked him. He had a ton of friends. He was one of the guys who picked on Noah.

"If you really think that will help the community, you can work on that," Mr. Young said. "But you will have to prove that it's helping."

"Can we look for ideas online?" Ethan asked.

"No," Mr. Young said. "I want to see what you come up with on your own. You can start brainstorming now."

For the rest of the class, Noah stared at a blank piece of paper. He listened to the clock ticking loudly.

What could he do? He couldn't think of one thing that would help the community.

He couldn't think of anything he could do, anyway. He was just a kid. He couldn't even drive. His dad let him drive the riding lawnmower, but that wasn't the same thing.

Noah sighed. He really wanted to give up.

What could a loser like me do to help out the community? he thought sadly.

After school, Noah walked home. It was a hot day.

I wish there was more shade, he thought. The sun beat down on him. Sweat dripped off his forehead.

At the end of the block, there was a big tree. *Maybe I can rest under that tree for a while*, Noah thought.

He tried to think about his project. Sitting under the tree, Noah wiped the sweat from his forehead. It was a lot cooler underneath the tree.

Then it hit him. The perfect project. It was something the community needed. It was something that the school needed. It was something that Noah needed.

More trees!

Chapter 3

At home, Noah had a snack. While he ate, he thought about his project. Even though he'd been working with his dad for nine years, he couldn't plant trees alone.

His dad always said it took a great team to do great work.

Noah found his dad in the kitchen, cooking something on the stove.

"Dad, how do you make a great team?" Noah asked.

Dad frowned. "What is the team going to do?" he asked.

"I have to do a project for school. I want to plant trees," Noah explained. "But I really can't do that all by myself."

"You're right," Dad said. "You'll need a team."

"How do I do that?" Noah asked.

Dad said, "The trick is to make it feel like the team is doing something fun. Not just working."

"Okay," Noah said. "Thanks for the help, Dad."

Now Noah knew exactly what to do. He had to make it cool to be on his team.

But how could he do that?

He went to his room and sat down at his desk. There was a sheet of white paper on the desk.

Noah picked up a green marker and started to draw a tree.

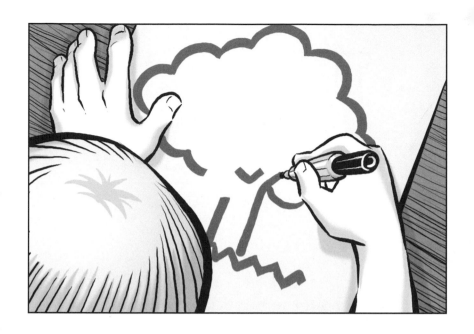

"Why would anyone join the Noah Green team?" he said to himself.

Then he stopped drawing. "The Green Team," Noah repeated. "That sounds pretty cool!"

Chapter 4

At school the next day, Noah hung up posters. The posters said, "Save the world. Join the Green Team! Friday after school."

By lunchtime, everyone was talking about the posters. As Noah walked through the cafeteria, he heard people whispering. "What do you think the Green Team is?" one girl asked another girl. "It sounds really cool."

At another table, Noah heard Ethan say, "So, what do you think will happen on Friday after school?"

Ethan's friend shook his head. "I don't know," he said, "but it sounds awesome. I'm definitely going to be there."

Noah smiled. He ate alone at lunch that day, but he felt better than he had felt in weeks.

After lunch, he stopped at the main office. He knocked on the door. The secretary, Ms. Fletch, smiled at him. "Come on in, Noah," she said. "Do you need to talk to Principal Loomis?"

"Yes," Noah said. "I wanted to ask him about a project I'm doing."

"Have a seat," Ms. Fletch said. "I'll tell him you're here." She walked into Principal Loomis's office.

Noah sat down on a hard, plastic chair. He waited. After a few minutes, Ms. Fletch came out of Principal Loomis's office. She smiled at Noah. "You can go in now," she said.

Inside the principal's office, Mr. Loomis was sitting behind his desk. "Hello, Noah," the principal said. "What can I do for you?"

Noah suddenly felt nervous. "Have you seen my signs around school, for the Green Team?" he asked.

Principal Loomis nodded. "Yes. I didn't know they were yours," he said. "What is the Green Team?"

Noah told the principal about the project in Mr. Young's class. "I need help planting trees," he explained. "So I thought a team would be a good way to do it."

"I'd like to be part of the team too. How can I help?" Principal Loomis asked.

Noah smiled. "I was hoping you'd
say that," he said. "I thought that
people could use a good reason to
plant trees. Maybe you could help me
come up with a reason."

Principal Loomis thought for a minute. Then he said, "I've got it! What if the kids who help plant the trees are allowed to eat their lunches outside?"

"That would be awesome!" Noah said. "They could sit next to the trees they planted."

"There wouldn't be much shade right away," Principal Loomis said. "But it would be a lot nicer than sitting in the cafeteria every day."

"Thanks," Noah said. "This is going to be great!"

Principal Loomis smiled. "See you after school on Friday, Noah," he said. "I'm glad I could help."

Chapter 5

After school, Noah stopped at his dad's landscape business. His dad was outside, loading some bags of dirt into a truck.

"Hey, Noah!" Dad said. "What are you doing here?"

"I was hoping that Green Thumb Landscaping would donate some trees to my project," Noah said. "We need about twenty trees."

Noah's dad smiled. "I think we can do that," he said. "It will be good for us, and good for the community too."

"Thanks, Dad!" Noah said, smiling. "Can you drop them off at school?"

"No problem. I'll bring the trees on Friday after school. Now get home and work on your homework!" Dad said. "See you later."

Chapter 6

A TRUCKLOAD OF TREES

In Social Studies class on Friday, Mr. Young asked Noah how his project was going.

"It's pretty good so far," Noah answered. "If you want to see the final project, you should come out to the flagpole after school today."

Mr. Young looked confused. "Okay," he said. "I'll be there."

The rest of the day went by slowly. Noah was excited and nervous about the Green Team's first meeting.

Would anyone show up? Would he and his dad have to plant twenty trees alone? He didn't know if someone would make fun of him, or try to wreck the project.

After school, he slowly walked outside. Some kids were leaving to walk home. Some were getting on the bus. But there was a group of at least forty kids waiting next to the flagpole. Mr. Young was there too, talking to Principal Loomis.

When Noah walked up, at first no one noticed. He felt invisible again. Then Principal Loomis saw him.

"Look, it's the leader of the Green Team!" the principal said.

"That kid is the leader?" Ethan said. He laughed. "This is lame."

Noah felt himself turn red.

"Tell us what the plan is, Noah," Mr. Young said.

Just then, Noah heard a truck pulling up behind him. He turned around. His dad's truck was parking next to the school. There were twenty small trees in the back.

"The Green Team is making our school greener," Noah explained.

"That's really lame," Ethan said.

"Yeah," another kid said. "We waited around all week for this?"

"Now, wait just a second," Principal Loomis said. "There's more."

Noah took a deep breath. "I noticed that there wasn't any shade here," he explained. "And to help our community and the environment, we can plant more trees here. Plus, Principal Loomis told me that everyone who helps out today gets to eat their lunches outside for the rest of the year."

"Is he telling the truth?" a girl asked Principal Loomis. "Do we really get to eat outside?"

"That's right," Principal Loomis said. "The trees won't give much shade now, but eating outside will be a lot better than eating inside."

All the kids waited to see what Ethan would say. Ethan just frowned.

"You don't have to do what Ethan does," Noah said quietly. "Even if he doesn't want to eat lunch outside, you still can if you're on the Green Team."

A girl nodded. "That would be so cool," she said.

Another girl agreed. "I would love to get out of that stinky cafeteria!" she said.

Ethan looked at the two girls. "I guess you're right," he said. "Eating outside is better than eating in the cafeteria. Okay, I'll stay."

Other kids agreed. Noah smiled. Everyone looked excited and happy. The project was working!

Noah's dad walked up, carrying a small tree and a shovel. "I've got apple trees and maple trees," he said. "Who wants to plant the first apple tree?"

One of the girls raised her hand. "Me!" she said. "But I don't know how. Noah, can you help me?"

Noah smiled and grabbed a shovel. "It's easy," he said.

Suddenly, Noah didn't feel so invisible anymore.

ABOUT THE AUTHOR

Jon Mikkelsen has written dozens of plays for kids, which have involved aliens, superheroes, and more aliens. He acts on stage and loves performing in front of an audience. Jon also loves sushi, cheeseburgers, and pizza. He loves to travel, and has visited Moscow, Berlin, London, and Amsterdam. He lives in Minneapolis and has a cat named Coco, who does not pay rent.

ABOUT THE ILLUSTRATOR

Nathan Lueth has been a freelance illustrator since 2004. He graduated from the Minneapolis College of Art and Design in 2004, and has done work for companies like Target, General Mills, and Wreked Records. Nathan was a 2008 finalist in Tokyopop's Rising Stars of Manga contest. He lives in Minneapolis, Minnesota.

GLOSSARY

community (kuh-MYOO-nuh-tee)—a group of people who live in the same area

donate (DOH-nate)—give something away, usually to help someone else

environment (en-VYE-ruhn-muhnt)—the natural world of the land, sea, and air

invisible (in-VIZ-uh-buhl)—something that cannot be seen

landscaping (LAND-skayp-ing)—a landscaping company works on outdoor projects at homes or businesses

popular (POP-yuh-lur)—liked or enjoyed by many people

project (PROJ-ekt)—a school assignment

respect (ri-SPEKT)—to admire someone

semester (suh-MESS-tur)—half of a school year

shade (SHAYD)—an area that is sheltered from the light

DISCUSSION QUESTIONS

1. Why does Noah feel invisible?

2. Does your school allow students to eat outside during lunch? What do you think about your school's rules during lunchtime?

3. Why does Ethan change his mind about joining the Green Team?

WRITING PROMPTS

1. Noah has to do a project to help the community. What would you do if you were given this assignment? How would you help your community?

2. If you had to come up with a name for a team, what would it be? Why?

3. In the summer, Noah works at his dad's landscaping company. What do you do in the summer? Write about it.

MORE ABOUT THE ENVIRONMENT

If you want to help the environment, planting a tree is one of the best things you can do.

Humans breathe in oxygen and breathe out carbon dioxide. But trees and other plants do the opposite. They take in carbon dioxide and release oxygen. Trees help make the air safe for humans and other animals to breathe.

First, if you want to plant a tree, you should get permission from the person who owns the land where you'll be planting the tree. It's also very important that they make sure there are no buried wires where you'll be planting.

Next, pick out your tree. A person at a home and garden store can help you find the right tree for the climate where you live. Although some trees won't grow in some climates, there are lots of trees to choose from.

You'll also need a tree that's the right size for the area where you're planting it. For example, a tree that will grow very big might not be the right choice for a small yard.

Finally, you're ready to plant your tree! Ask the person who sells you the tree to give you tips for planting it. Some trees require special food or handling while they're being placed in the ground.

Remember to water your tree right away. Lots of water will help your tree thrive in its new location.

You might want to make a schedule for caring for the tree. Some trees need extra care, like trimming. You can ask the person at the home and garden store for more information about your tree.

Congratulations! By planting a tree and taking care of it, you've done something great for your neighborhood, your community, and the environment.

Sometimes it just takes a small step to do a great thing!

INTERNET SITES

Do you want to know more about subjects related to this book? Or are you interested in learning about other topics? Then check out FactHound, a fun, easy way to find Internet sites.

Our investigative staff has already sniffed out great sites for you!

Here's how to use FactHound:

1. Visit *www.facthound.com*

2. Select your grade level.

3. To learn more about subjects related to this book, type in the book's ISBN number: **9781434207890**.

4. Click the **Fetch It** button.

FactHound will fetch the best Internet sites for you!